POLLY AND THE PUFFIN

Jenny Colgan

Polly and the Puffin

LB

The New Friend

LITTLE, BROWN BOOKS FOR YOUNG READERS

First published in Great Britain in 2017 by Hodder and Stoughton

1 3 5 7 9 10 8 6 4 2

A CIP catalogue record for this book is available from the British Library.

ISBN 9781510200906

Printed in China
The paper and board used in this book are made from wood from responsible sources.

For Ron

This is a story about Polly, a girl who lives in a little house by the sea.

She has a puffin friend.
His name is Neil.

Polly was starting something she calls "Big School", although you might call it something else.

She was not happy about it. At all. Neil wasn't allowed to come!

"I think you're going to love school," her mummy said.

"But I love everything how it is now," said Polly.

"I know," said Mummy.

"Can I wear my spotty wellingtons?" said Polly, staring at her new black shoes. She didn't like them.

"No," said Mummy gently.

"Don't forget your snack for playtime!" Mummy said as they were leaving.

"Hang on. Have you got Neil in your rucksack?"

"No," said Polly.

"Eep!" said Nobody Who Was In The Rucksack.

"Neil can come and play when you get back from school," said Mummy.

"I have a bad feeling about this," said Polly.

"You will have a great time and make lots of new friends!" said Polly's mummy.

Polly thought for a moment.

"Make Neil a cake in case he misses me too much. But don't let him eat it all. Maybe I can have some leftover cake when I get back. Also, he likes chocolate cake but he says coffee cake is yuck, yuck, YUCK."

"All right," said Polly's mummy, and gave her a big cuddle, just like this one I am giving you now. "You're going to have such fun!"

Polly felt so, so sad.

Her mummy felt so, so sad.

"Yes," said Polly in her smallest voice.

They walked along the harbour wall, but Polly didn't jump up on it as she usually did. Instead, she dragged the toes of her shoes on the cobbles.

"I also think," said Polly, "you should not have another baby while I am at school."

"OK, I won't do that," said Mummy.

"Good," said Polly. "Because, you know. You already have me and Neil. And that is Quite Enough."

"I agree," said Mummy. "Also, shoes are expensive."

Polly had a teacher. Her name was Miss Wing. She had long dark hair and a green hat.

There were other boys and girls there. Polly had seen them before, at the beach and at the playpark. But now they all looked different and they all had new shoes and some of them were crying.

Polly didn't like this one bit.

The other children were called: Arun, Bridget, Ronita, Marius, Charles, Kelsie, Francesco, Lauren, Vivi, Kit, Mohammed, Holly, Dillon, Francis, Evie, Florence, Agnieska, Hugo, Matilda, Barney, Celia, Oscar, Sybella and Sophia.

Miss Wing

They played at the water table.
Polly wasn't sure what to do.

They played in the sandpit.
Polly wasn't sure what to do.

They did some painting. (If you would like to know how to draw Neil, you can learn at the back of this book.)

They had playtime.

Miss Wing noticed Polly standing alone in the playground. She brought Ronita over.

"Perhaps you two could make friends?" she said cheerfully.

Polly looked at Ronita. Ronita looked at Polly.

It is not so easy to make friends just like that. They didn't talk to each other for a little while.

"I have dungarees," said Ronita finally.

"Oh," said Polly. "I have a bird. At home."

"I have a bird!" said Ronita.

"No you don't," said Polly. "*I* have a bird."

"Yes I DO!" Ronita raised her voice.

"No you DON'T!" Polly raised hers back.

"YES I DO ACTUALLY I HAVE THE BEST BIRD IN THE WORLD!" Ronita shouted.

"Now, everybody settle down," said Miss Wing nicely, because she was the nice kind of teacher.

"My bird is the best in the world," said Polly, quietly. "He's a puffin."

"Mine is a green-winged macaw. You probably don't know, but that's a parrot."

And then Polly was cross, and said something that later she wished she hadn't.

"That sounds rubbish," she said.

They didn't talk again after that.

"How was school?" said Mummy as they got home. "Look! I made a chocolate cake!"

"I don't want any," said Polly.

"Oh," said Mummy. "That bad?"

"Where's Neil?" Polly sniffed.

"I think he's gone to his nest at the lighthouse."

Polly started to cry. Mummy brought over some cake anyway, in case it would help. (It was warm.)

"What happened?"

"There was a girl there," said Polly. "WITH ANOTHER BIRD."

"Oh dear," said Mummy. "That does sound bad."

"Also," said Polly. "I need dungarees."

It was hard, going to school.

Polly tried to play with the others at playtime.

"We're playing 'Parrot Tag'," said one of the girls. "But you think parrots are rubbish. So maybe you shouldn't play with us."

Polly didn't know what to say about that. So she walked away and stood very quietly all by herself.

The next day, Polly pretended to have a tummy ache.

She didn't want to play tug-of-war with Neil.

She didn't want to play splash ball either.

She didn't even want to do the funky boogaloo to the sounds of the radio.

Mummy had to do it. And Mummy was TERRIBLE at it.

Polly stomped off.
Neil followed her.

Mummy looked for them all over the house.

Finally, she found them. Polly had made a nest for herself and Neil under the covers.

"Eep," said Neil in a very, very small voice.

"Polly?" said Mummy.

"Eep," said Polly. "I think I am going to be a puffin and live in a nest. Thank you, Mummy. I don't need to go to Big School any more."

"Ah," said Mummy. "Well, I think I am going to talk to Miss Wing."

Miss Wing listened to Mummy and made a suggestion.

"What's going to happen?" asked Polly.

"Miss Wing suggested you bring Neil to school. And Ronita is going to bring her parrot, Skittles."

"Yay!" said Polly.

"I think Miss Wing is quite a new teacher," said Mummy.

Polly was very excited about taking Neil to school.

As a special treat, she let him sleep in his box inside.

And in the morning they ate special cereal (the kind that is normally for the weekend).

When they'd finished, Polly wanted to put a tie on Neil so he'd look smart. Neil did not want that.

Mummy was coming too, as the birds were "Show and Tell".

In the classroom, Polly looked at Ronita.

Neil looked at Skittles.

He was a very big parrot. He was quite cool.

"Eep," said Neil.

Polly was about to tell Ronita her parrot WAS a good bird after all, and to say sorry, when . . .

The two birds flew up into the air!

CRASH!!

Skittles and Neil raced around the classroom. They knocked over the paints and scattered the books.

Skittles grabbed Miss Wing's green hat. Then Neil grabbed the other side.

Miss Wing shouted at the birds but they didn't listen, they just kept playing tug of war with her hat!

Polly looked at Ronita.
Ronita looked at Polly.
And they both started to laugh!

Polly got Neil down with some of the bun Mummy had given her for playtime.

And Ronita got Skittles down with some of the dates her mummy had given her for playtime.

Bringing the birds to school had been a disaster! The mummies had to take them home.

The mummies' faces were like this:

"No more birds in the classroom," said Miss Wing. "I thought they would be friends."

She looked at the girls.

"It's hard to make friends," said Polly quietly.

"I think so too," said Ronita.

"Well then," said Miss Wing. "Aren't you two lucky you've already done it?"

When Ronita came over to play, they found they didn't just like birds.

Ronita liked pizza. Polly liked pizza!

Ronita liked cereal. Polly liked cereal!

Ronita liked dollies. Polly liked racoons!

So they played racoon dollies.

Mummy watched them.

"Why do you have a sad face, Mummy?" asked Polly. "I love Big School now. I have lots of friends!"

"I know," said Mummy. "I'm just watching you grow up. Which is a happy thing, but it happens so fast."

Mummy went off to fetch them some cake, in the little house by the sea. And everything was calm.

Except for Neil and Skittles of course. They HATED each other!

RECIPES

Polly and Neil's Favourite Chocolate Cake

This is the cake that Polly's mummy likes to make for special occasions, for friends or if Polly just needs cheering up. You will need a grown-up to help with this recipe, especially when putting the cake in the oven.

INGREDIENTS

For the cake:

- 2 tablespoons of cocoa
- 4 tablespoons of hot water
- 225g butter (make sure this is at room temperature before you start)
- 225g caster sugar
- 4 eggs
- 225g self-raising flour

For the icing:

- 225g plain chocolate
- 100g butter

Optional decorations:

Chocolate buttons, hundreds and thousands, cherries . . . use your imagination!

INSTRUCTIONS

1. Grease two 20cm baking tins and set the oven to 180°C.
2. Put the cocoa into a small bowl and add the hot water. Mix until smooth.
3. Put the butter, sugar, eggs and flour into a large bowl and beat well. Once mixed, add the cocoa mixture and stir.
4. Divide the mixture between your two tins and put them in the oven. You'll need to bake the cake for 25 minutes. (TIP: you can test the cake with a fork – if the mixture sticks to the fork it's not done yet, if it comes out clean the cake is ready!)
5. Remove the cake from the tins and allow to cool on a wire rack.

6. For the icing, melt the chocolate and butter in a heat-resistant bowl over a saucepan of hot water. Make sure the two are mixed well.
7. Place one half of the cake on a plate, and spread half of your icing on it. (TIP: work from the centre outwards.)
8. Then put the other half of the cake on top, and use the remaining icing to cover the outside.
9. You can decorate the cake in any pattern you like before eating!

Flapjack for Playtime

Polly and Ronita's parents are very good at making nice snacks. Mostly that means carrot sticks or an apple, but sometimes that means flapjack! This recipe is very easy, but you'll need a grown-up to help you with using the oven and the hob.

INGREDIENTS

- 40g dried fruit (raisins, prunes and apricots all work really well, but you can you choose your favourite)
- 40g seeds (Neil thinks sunflower seeds and pumpkin seeds are a good choice)
- 130g oats
- 100g butter
- 3 tablespoons golden or maple syrup

INSTRUCTIONS

1. Measure all the dry ingredients and mix in a bowl.
2. Ask a grown-up to gently melt the butter and syrup together in a saucepan for you.
3. When melted, the grown-up should remove the pan from the heat and pour the butter-syrup into the oats, seeds and fruit mix.
4. Give it all a good stir!

5. Take a small oven-proof dish or baking tray and line it with baking paper (no need to grease it – the mixture is already nice and buttery!).
6. Transfer your oat mix into the dish and get your grown-up to put it in the oven for 20 minutes at 160°C.

7. You will need to allow the flapjack to cool completely before cutting into slices otherwise it will crumble (although Polly says that she likes it best when it's warm and crumbly...).

POLLY AND NEIL

DO NOT

Parrots!

Did you know . . .?

There are over 350 species of parrot.

The smallest parrot is only 8.5 cm tall.

The biggest parrot is almost as tall as Polly!

In the wild, parrots usually live in flocks of 20 to 30 birds.

Some parrots can live for up to 80 years.

Parrot Jokes

Q: What do you get when you cross a parrot and a shark?

A: A bird
that talks your ear off!

Q: What do you call a parrot that flies away?

A: A polygon!

Q: How do you help a sick parrot?

A: With medical tweetment!

Q. What's orange and sounds like a parrot?

A. A carrot!

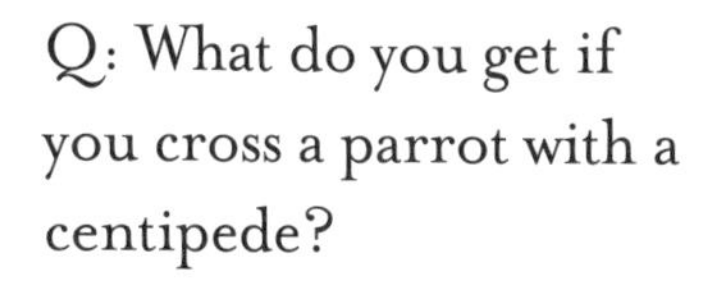

Q: What do you get if you cross a parrot with a centipede?

A: A walkie-talkie!

ACTIVITIES

How to Draw Neil

1 Draw a big circle for Neil's body.

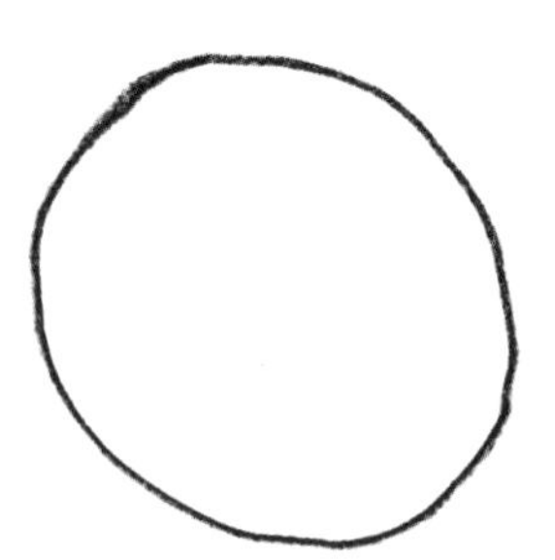

2 Draw a small circle for Neil's head.

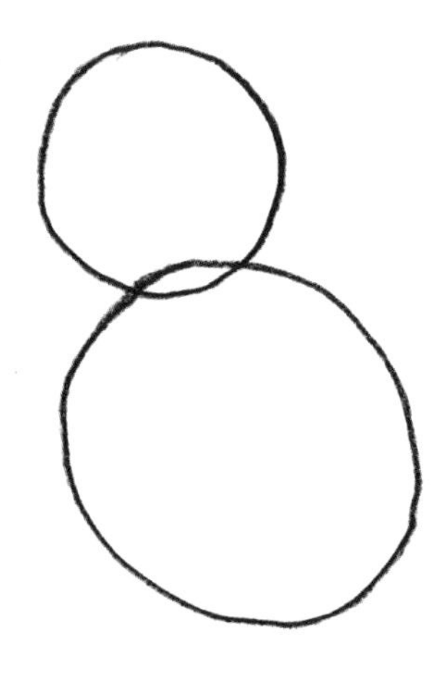

3 Draw a triangle for Neil's beak.

4 Add his legs and feet.

5 Colour in a black half moon shape on the back of Neil's head.

6 Add some black wings on his body.

7 All that is left now is to add his eyes!

Spot the Difference

Can you spot the three differences between these two parrots? Maybe you could colour them in afterwards!

Polly and Ronita's Home-Made Phone

Did you know that you can make your own phone to speak on with your friend? This is something your parents might remember making when they were little, too . . .

You will need:

- Two plastic cups (the kind you use at parties and picnics)
- A long piece of string
- A sharp pencil

How to make the phone:

1. Ask a grown-up to make a hole in the bottom of each cup with the pencil.
2. Thread the string through each hole, using blue tack or sticky tape to keep it in place.

3. Take one cup each, and stand as far away from each other as the string will reach.
4. Now, take it in turns to speak into your cup quietly, while your friend holds the other cup to their ear. Magically, you'll be able to hear each other!

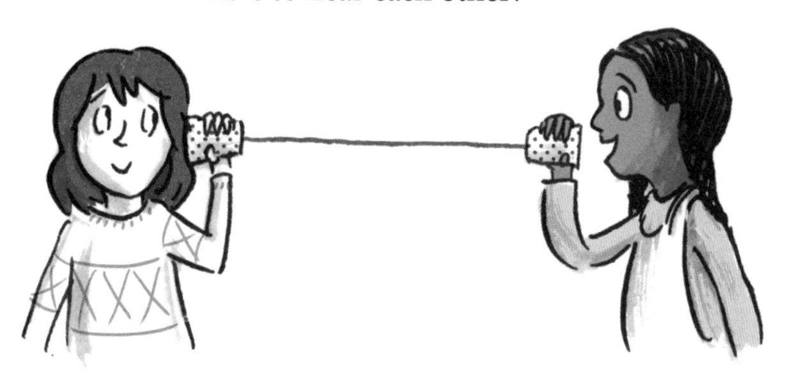

Ronita's top tips:

1. It's good to speak into your phone like it's a walkie-talkie – when you finish speaking say 'over!' so that your friend knows it's their turn to talk.
2. Skittles is not very good at squawking quietly when it's his turn . . .

Jenny Colgan is best known for writing bestselling novels for grown-ups including *Meet Me at the Cupcake Café* and *Welcome to Rosie Hopkins' Sweetshop of Dreams.* But when a feathery character from *Little Beach Street Bakery* caught her readers' attention she knew he needed a story of his own . . .

Thomas Docherty is an acclaimed author and illustrator of children's picture books including *Little Boat, Big*

Scary Monster and *The Driftwood Ball*. *The Snatchabook*, which was written by his wife Helen, has been shortlisted for several awards in the UK and the US and translated into 17 languages. He loves going into schools and helping kids to write their own stories. Thomas lives in Wales by the sea with his wife and two young daughters, so he had plenty of inspiration when it came to illustrating *Polly and the Puffin*.

Neil can't believe he's in so many books now! He has a cameo in several of Jenny's adult books, and three with Polly. Their fourth book will be out in time for Christmas. (Polly and Neil *love* Christmas.)

Have you read Polly and Neil's other books?